The Water Park

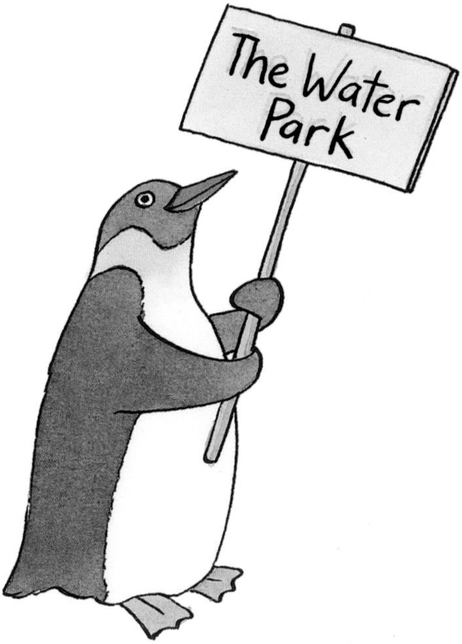

Illustrated by Trevor Pye

Rigby

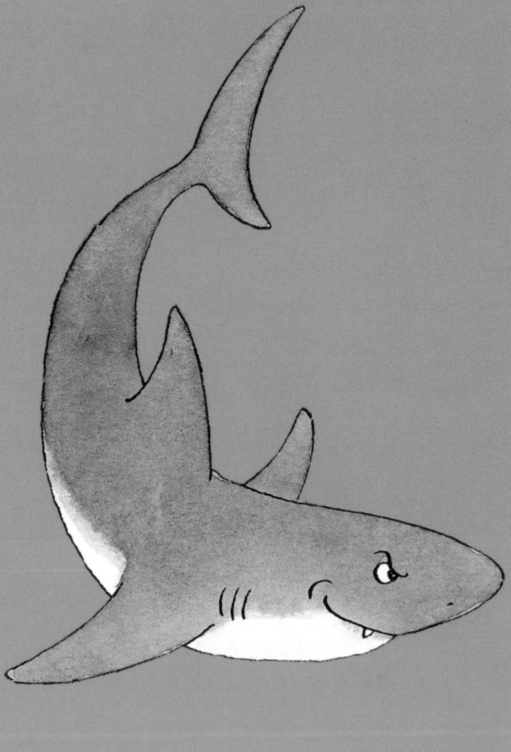

Here is the shark.

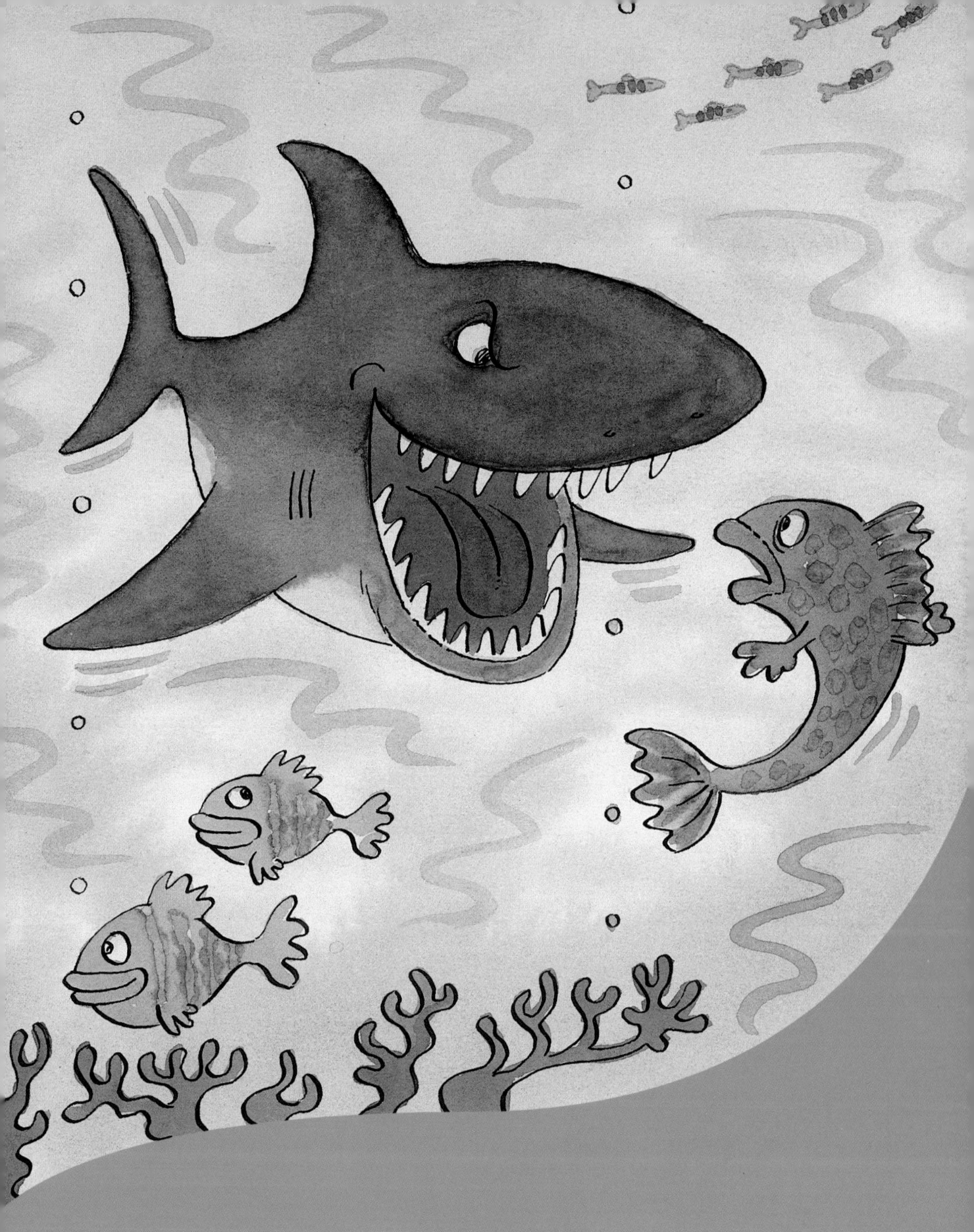

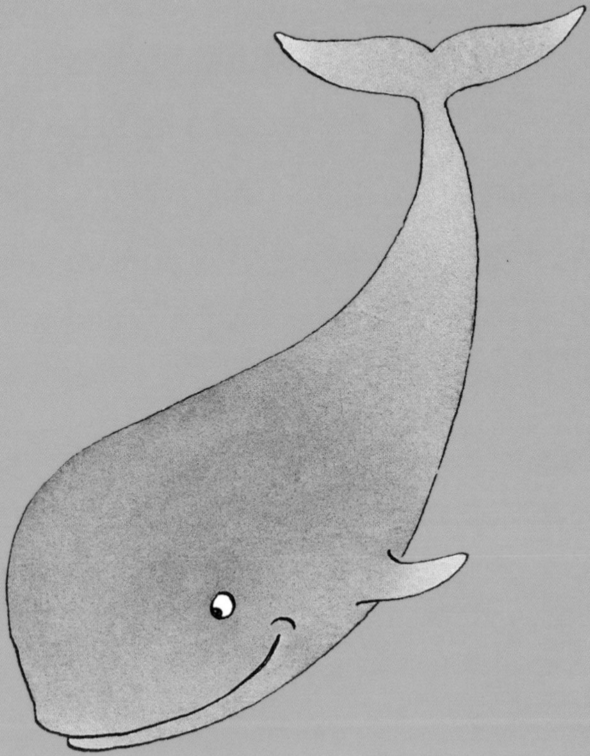

Here is the whale.

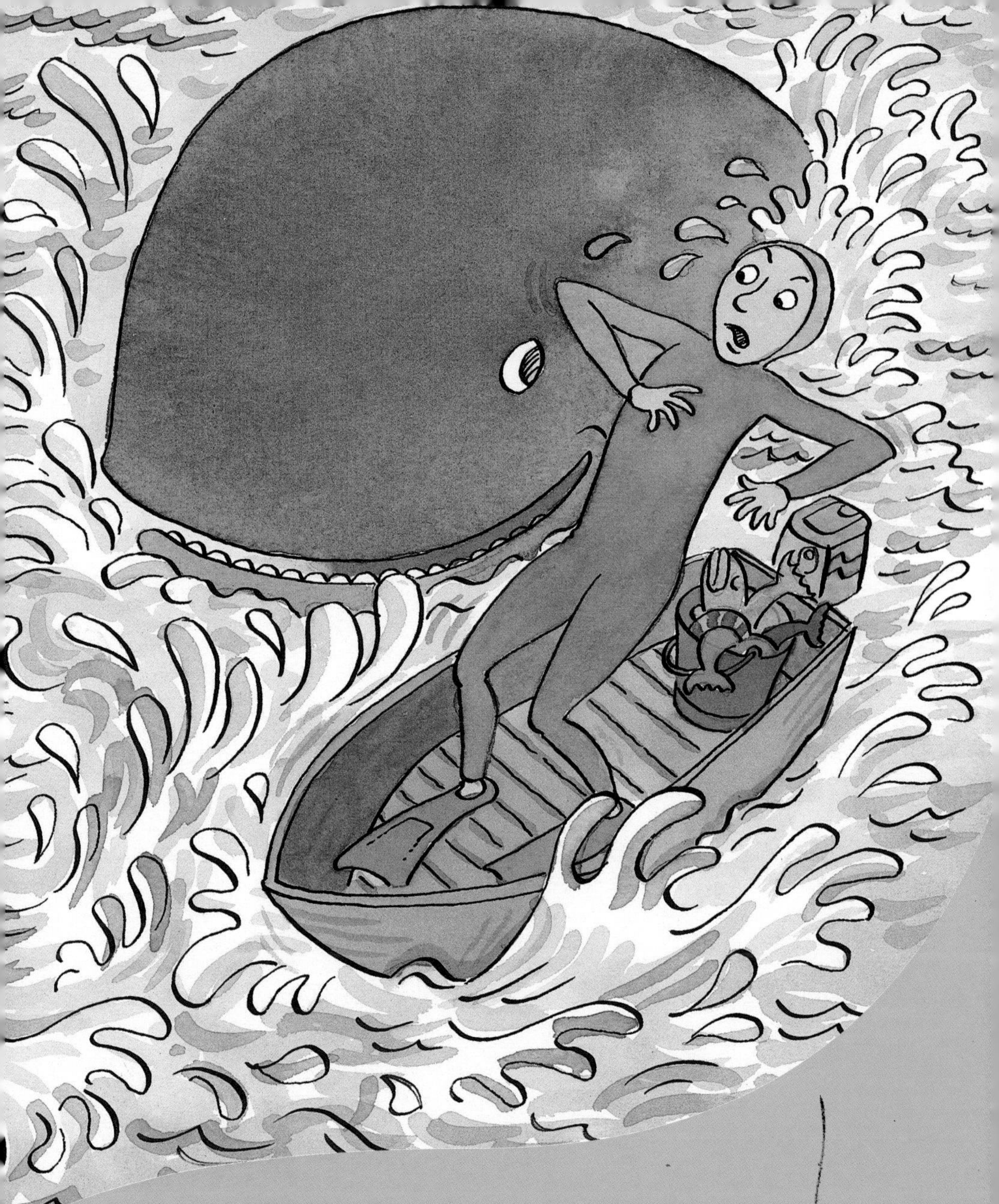

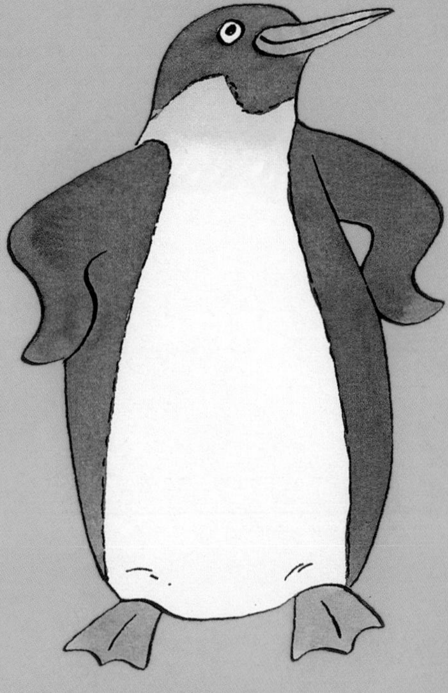

Here is the penguin.

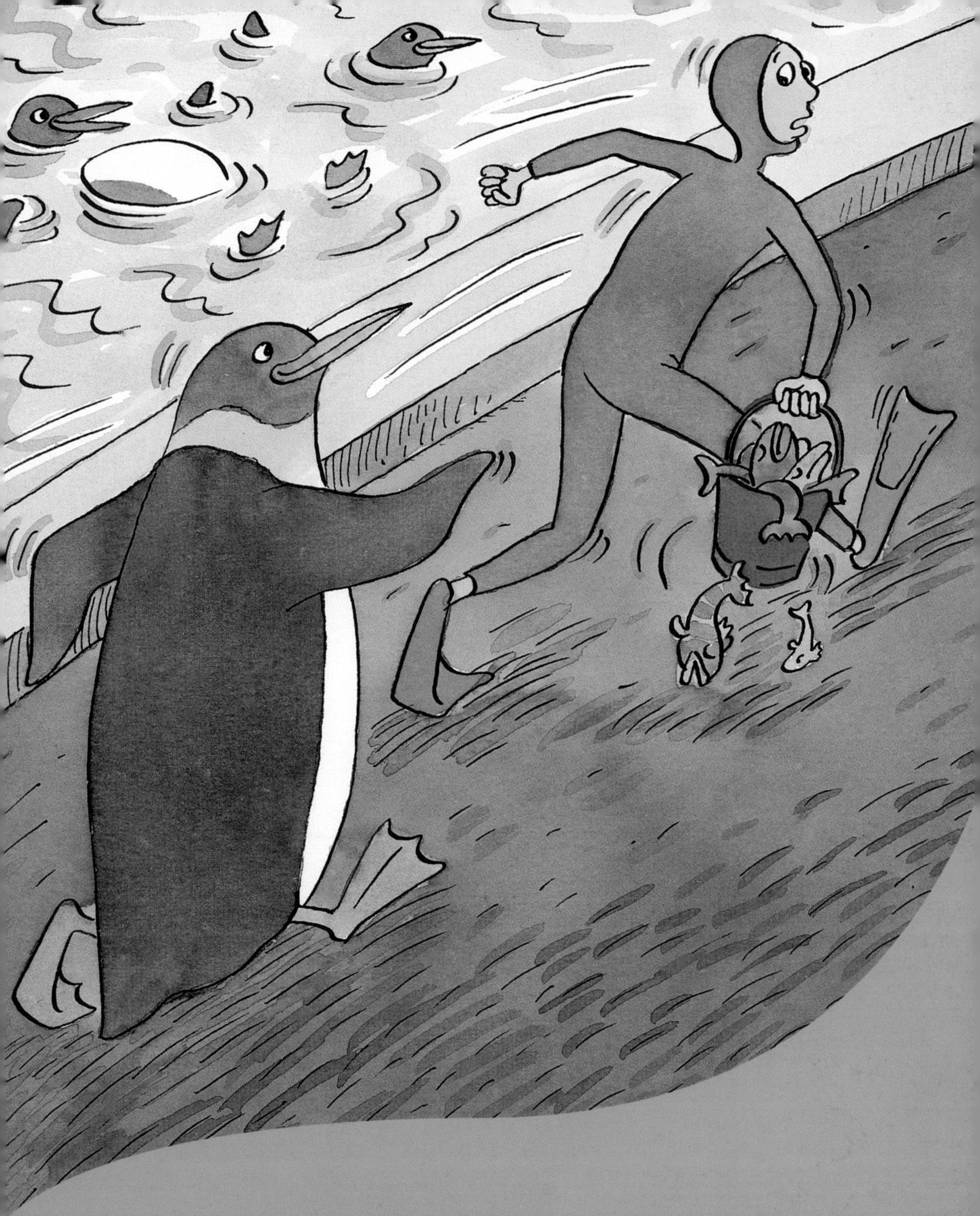

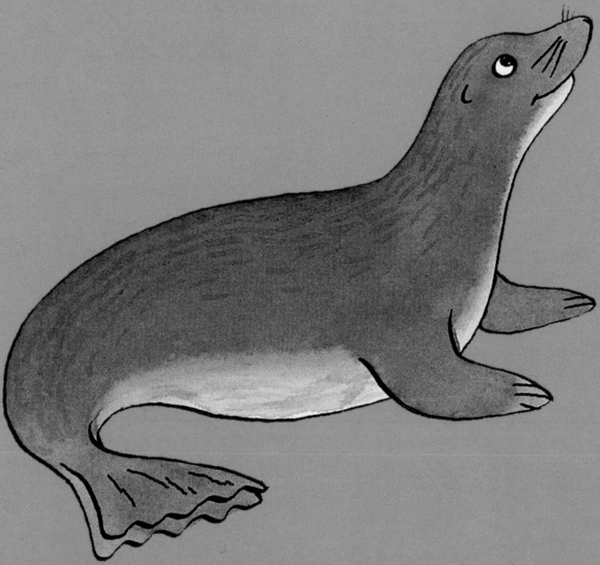

Here is the seal.

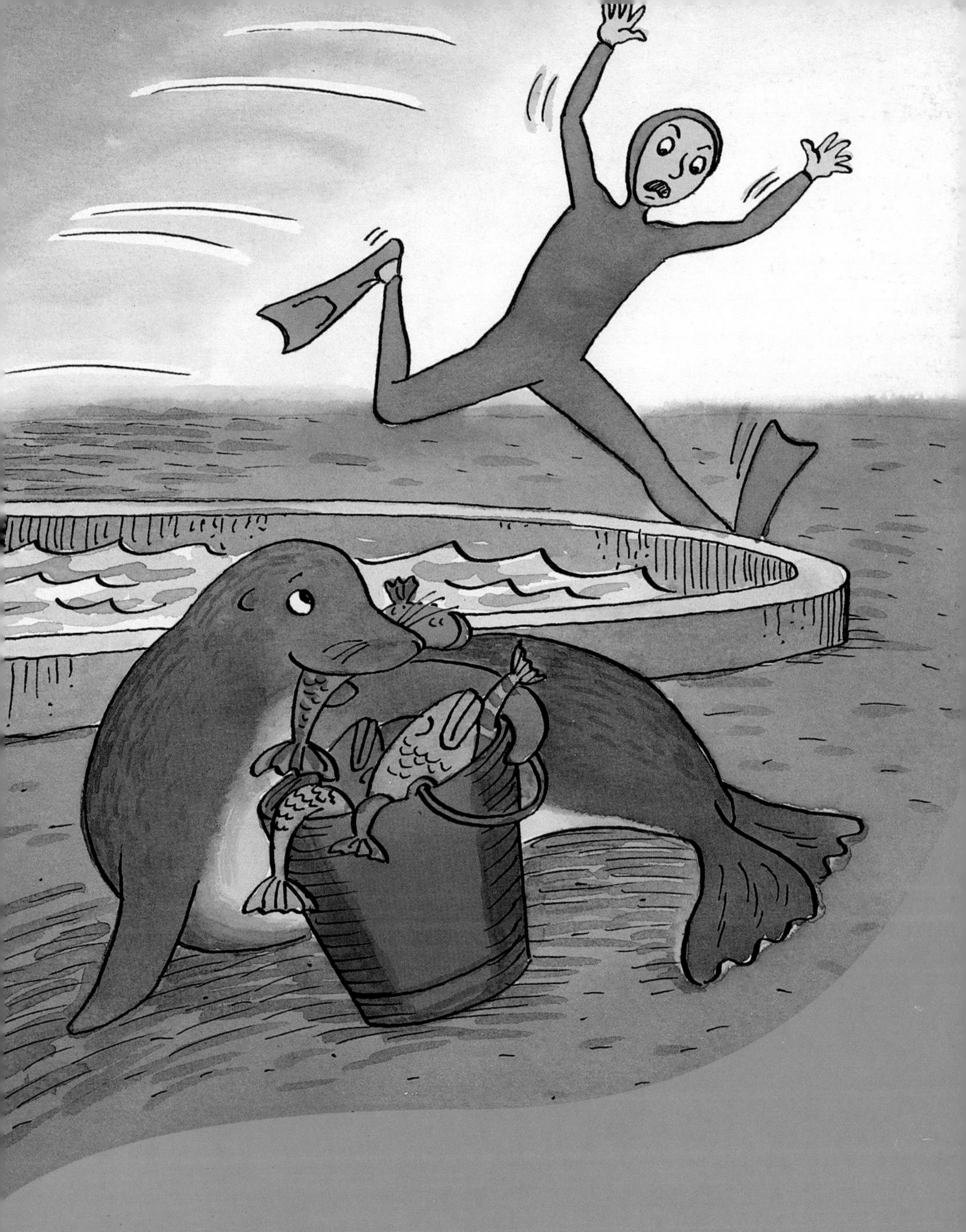

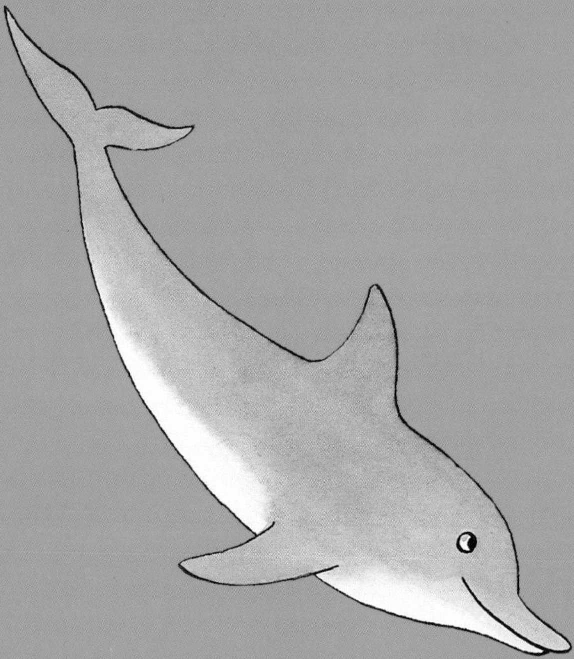

Here is the dolphin.

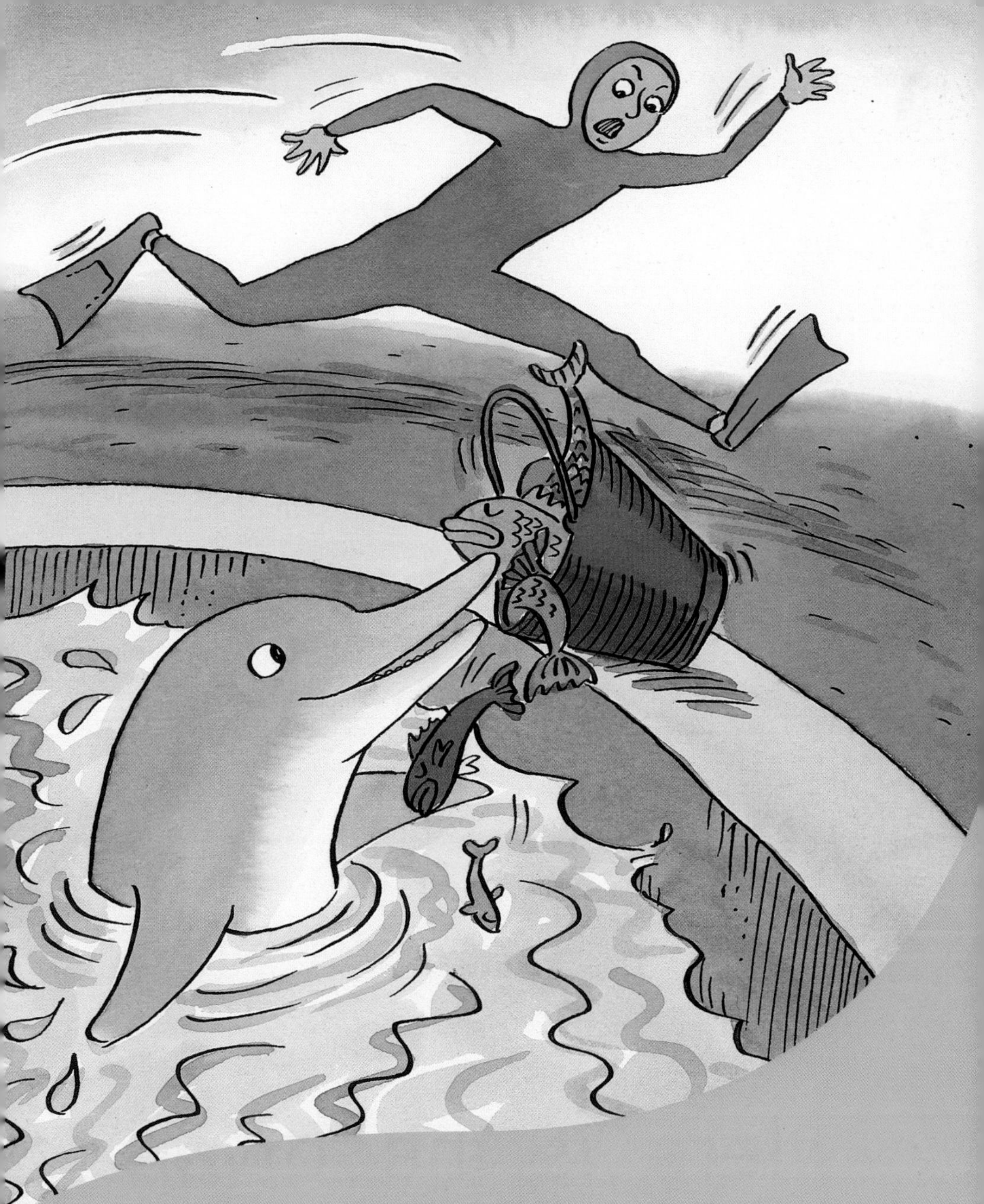

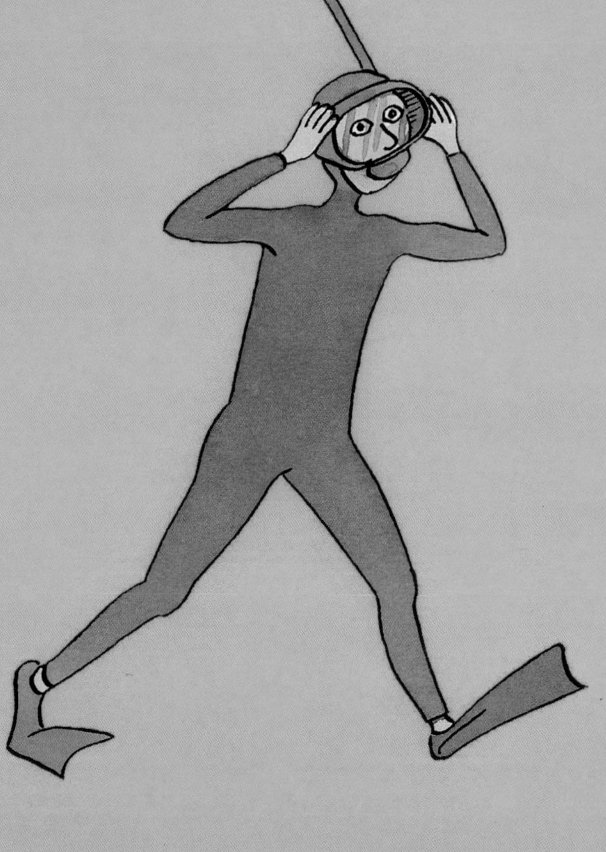

Here is the diver.

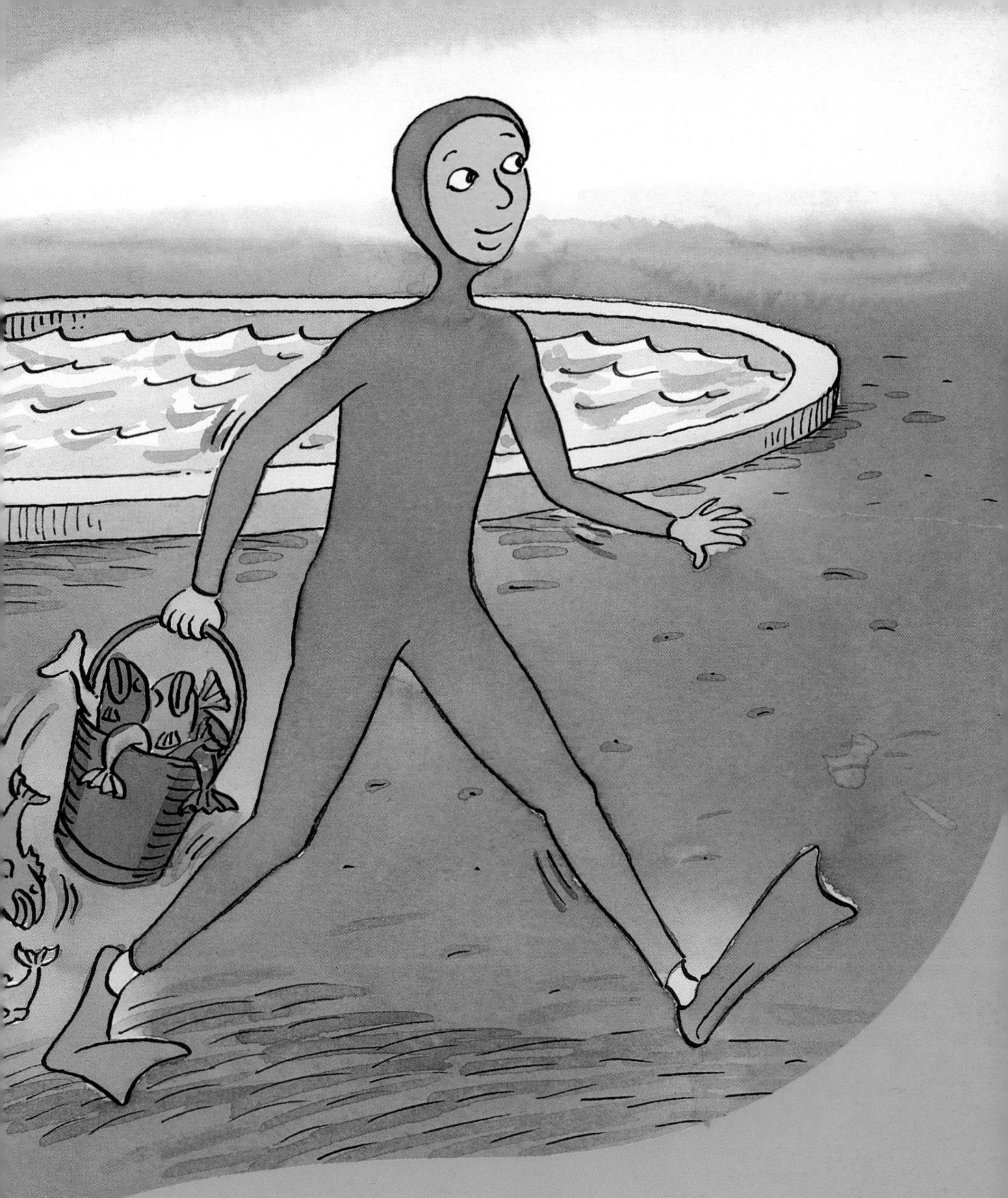

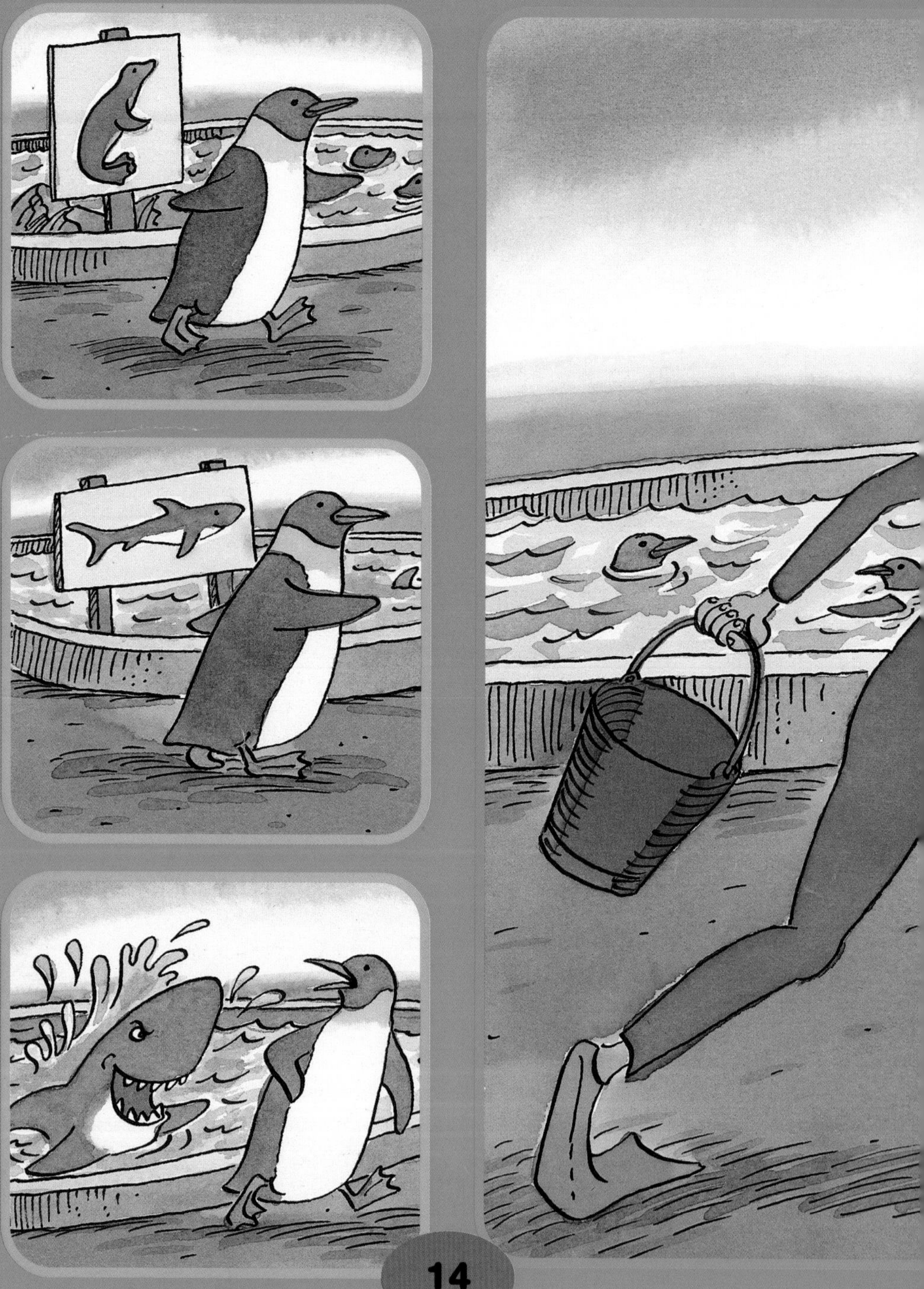

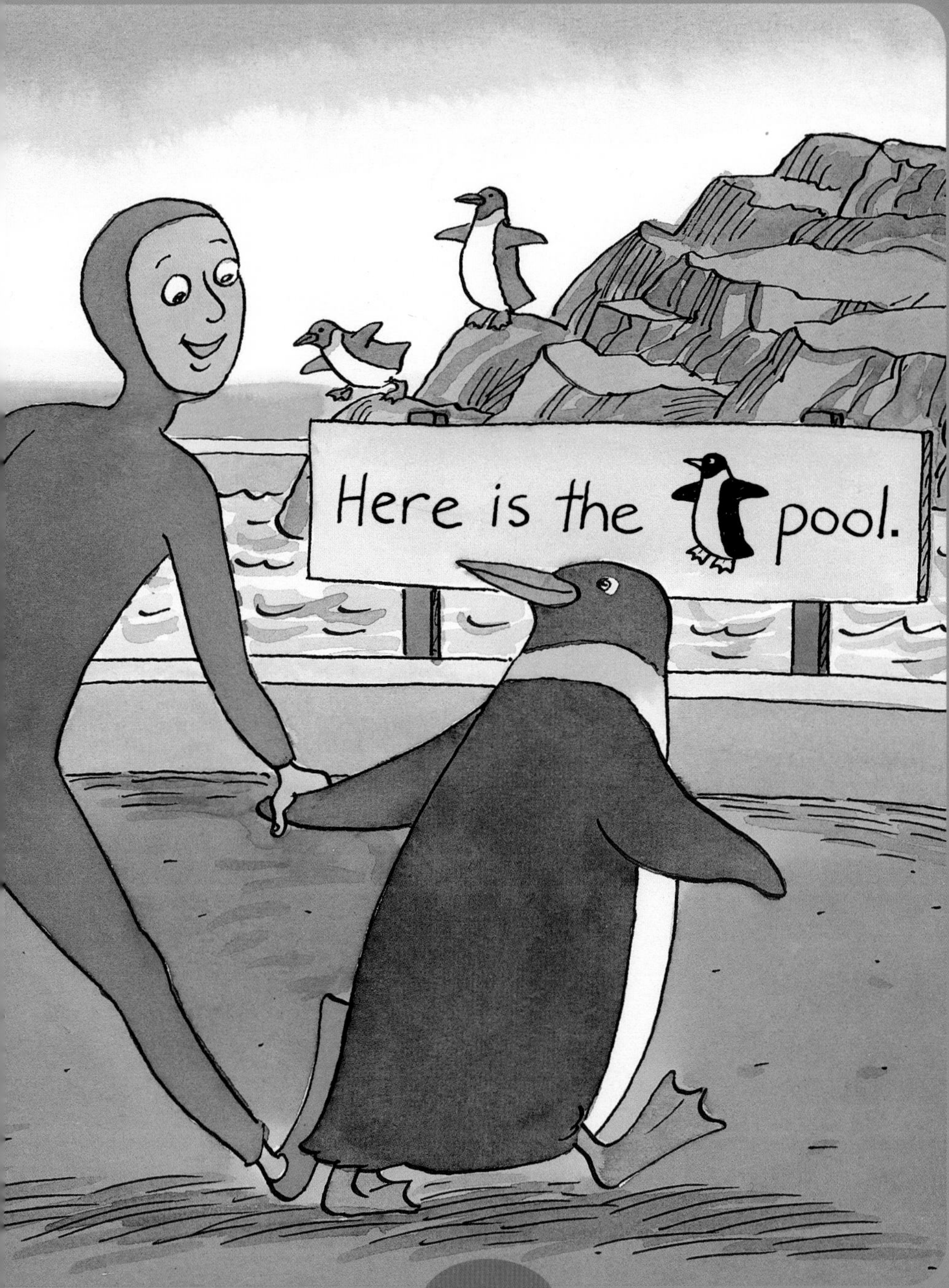
Here is the pool.

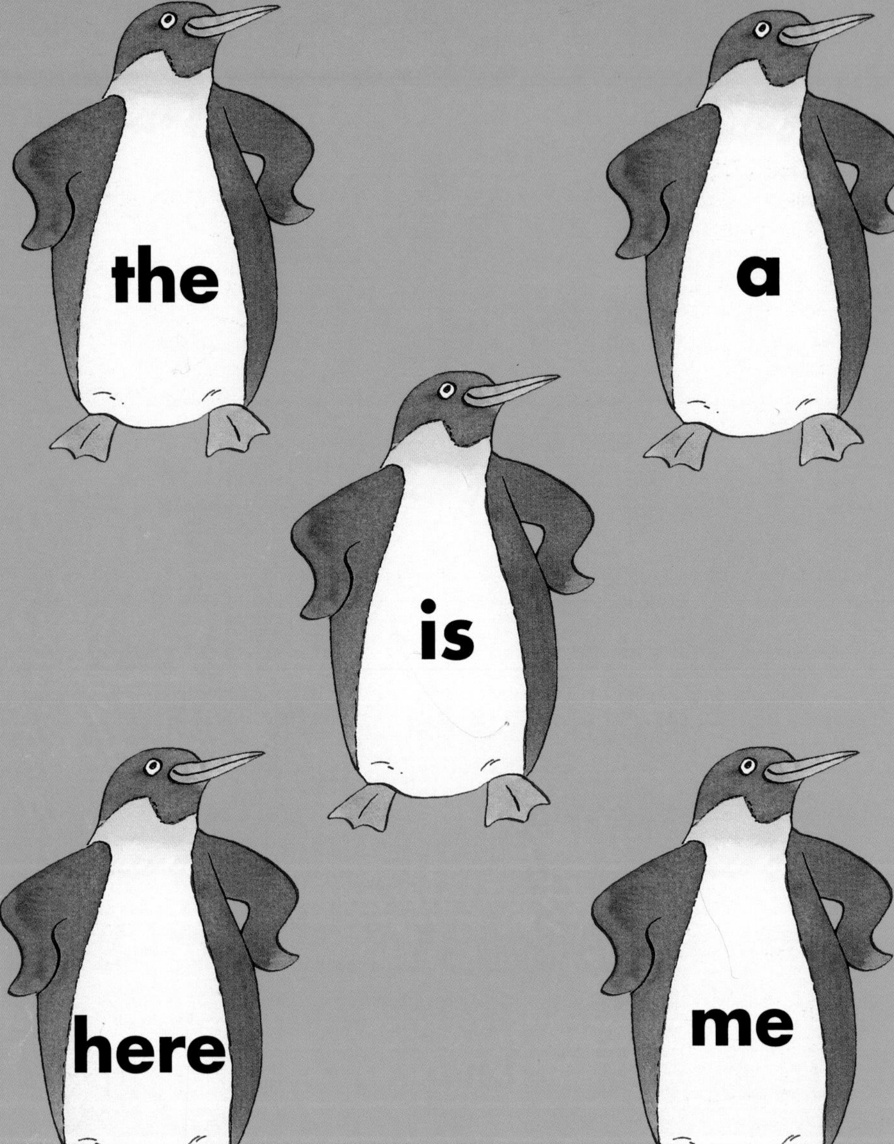
the
a
is
here
me